For Joseph & Jeannette

THE BIRD WHO WAS AFRAID TO CLEAN THE CROCODILE'S TEETH!

by
PARIS & TAYLOR™

This is a story about some birds who *cannot* fly.

Cleaning the teeth of crocodiles is *how* they get by!

It is the *way* these birds *earn* their daily meal.

Clean teeth is *what* the crocs get from the deal!

This leaves both parties just as happy as could be.

The birds get fed and the crocs' dental work is free!

Every bird had to keep *one* crocodile's teeth clean.

Slim had Gar, the *meanest* looking croc he'd seen!

Gar's face had *warts*! His teeth were *dark* yellow!

He had a *giant* scar! He was a *scary* looking fellow!

Scared to clean Gar's teeth, Slim had *not* eaten in a while.

And he had to listen to rumors about the crocodile!

Looking at their watches, the birds moved away from land.

Each one had their toothbrush and dental pick in hand.

Everyone *except* for our friend Slim.

He tried to hide while the croc *stared* at him!

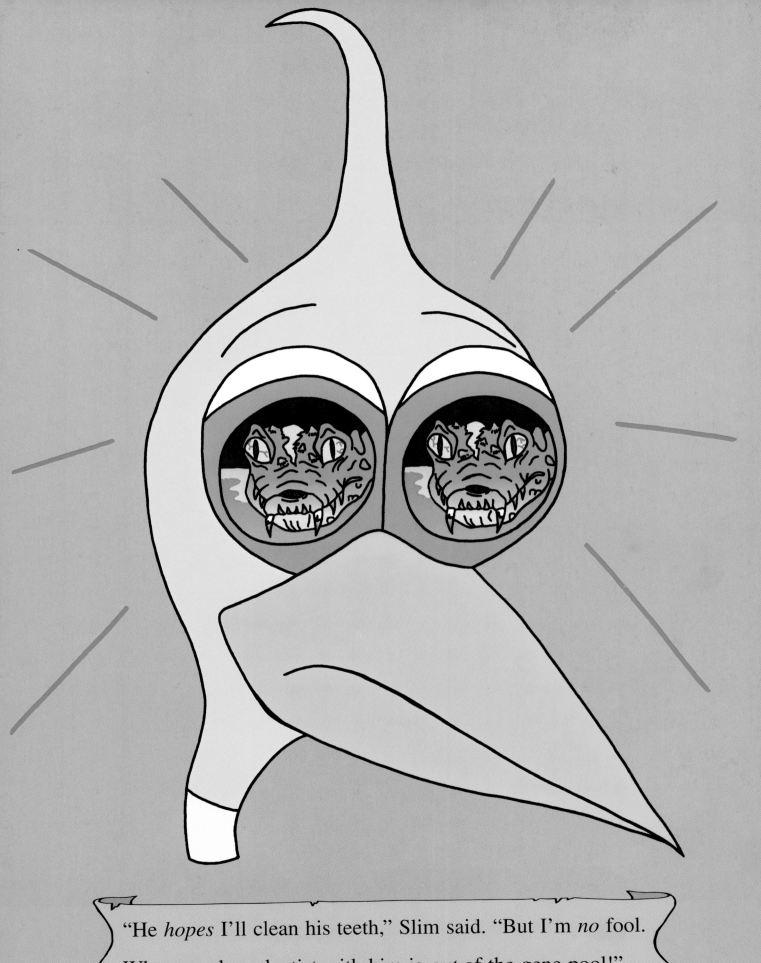

"He *hopes* I'll clean his teeth," Slim said. "But I'm *no* fool. Whoever plays dentist with him is *out* of the gene pool!"

Everyone fell asleep with a smile on their face.

Except for Slim who watched Gar float in place.

"Tomorrow, I'll look in the jungle for something to eat.

Maybe," he said, "I'll find some roots or wild wheat!"

"That food *isn't* right for me. I'll get a bellyache!

But I'll have to live with it. My *life* is at stake!"

The next day Slim looked into the jungle. He was scared.

"I hope the mosquitoes *don't* give me malaria," he declared.

"Maybe I *won't* get a disease if I don't go *too* far.

Oh well," he said, "it's *this* or a *hot* date with Gar!"

He searched but could *not* find anything to eat.

All that he got was *tired* and *sore* feet!

He was right. Somebody *was* watching him.
A friendly looking cat was looking at Slim!

"A bird who *can't* fly is something I *don't* see every day.

It looks like," the cat laughed, "I found some *easy* prey!"

"I *can't* hear you," Slim said. "I'm *too* far away."

"Well, move closer," the cat said. "What do you say?"

The panther did not have to wait long at that.

Within seconds, Slim had reached the cat.

The panther said, "You fell for it, hook, line and sinker!

When it comes to brains, you're *not* a deep thinker!"

"I'm sorry," Slim said, "I *don't* understand."

"You will!" the cat snarled. Some claws *sprang* from his hand!

"Trusting that panther," Slim said, "is *something* I regret!
I'll be safe if I reach the river for cats *hate* to get wet!"

Gar swam up to Slim. He noticed the bird was in trouble!

"Hop on and I'll *save* you!" the croc said. "On the double!"

Slim was surprised to be safe and sound.
Gar had ferried him away from dry ground!

"Don't get me wrong," Slim said. "I'm not one who complains.
But I should be dead, with my kin trying to identify my remains!"

Hurt by Slim's remark, Gar was sad and confused.

"Why on earth would I eat my dentist?" he mused.

"You look *so* mean," Slim said, "that it makes sense."

"I see," Gar said, "you judged me on my appearance."

"Now hold on a minute," the bird questioned Gar.

"What about all those stories? *What* about that scar?"

"But the crocs *also* avoid you," Slim said with a sigh.

"How do you explain that? What's the reason why?"

"The reason," the crocodile said, "I'm *avoided* by my chums,

Is I have *bad breath* because you're *afraid* to clean my gums!"

Slim knew he was wrong and *knew* what to do.

"I'm sorry Gar," he said, "for prejudging you.

For someone's looks can often hide

Just who that someone *really* is inside!"

"I also thought the cat wouldn't hurt me.

Only because he *looked* so friendly."

Being as kind hearted as a crocodile could be,

Gar understood and accepted Slim's apology.

Today, our pal has a toothpick hanging out of his beak.

His name's still Slim but it *doesn't* match his physique!

His belly is four sizes bigger than it *ever* used to be.

He eats the stuff from Gar's teeth, *never* going hungry!

He cleans the croc's teeth three times, each and every day,

Keeping Gar's pearly whites *free* of plaque and tooth decay!

With his *shiny* teeth, Gar now sports a smile a mile wide.

Minus his *bad breath*, his fellow crocs are by his side!

THE END!

The birds learned not to judge someone on their appearance.

Doing so, *without* knowing them first, *doesn't* make sense!

CHECK LIST PAGE!

Check off the book you have!

Visit our web site at: www.parisandtaylor.com

You have my book! Now get the rest! They're Great!

THE WORLD'S GREATEST CHILDREN'S BOOKS!™

- ☐ THE ELEPHANT WHO COULDN'T REMEMBER!
- ☐ THE TURTLE WHO FELT BOXED IN!
- ☐ THE BIRD WHO DIDN'T WANT TO FLY SOUTH FOR THE WINTER!
- ☑ THE BIRD WHO WAS AFRAID TO CLEAN THE CROCODILE'S TEETH!
- ☐ THE BEAR WHO COULDN'T HIBERNATE! (SLEEP)
- ☐ THE STRAW THAT DIDN'T BREAK THE CAMEL'S BACK!
- ☐ THE SKUNK WHO DIDN'T WANT TO STINK!
- ☐ THE OPOSSUM WHO DIDN'T WANT TO PLAY DEAD ANYMORE!
- ☐ THE PENGUIN WHO HATED THE COLD BECAUSE HE WAS ALL DRESSED UP AND HAD NO PLACE TO GO!
- ☐ THE ROOSTER WHO DIDN'T WANT TO WAKE UP EARLY ANYMORE!
- ☐ THE PIG WHO DIDN'T WANT TO GET DIRTY!
- ☐ THE LEMMING WHO DIDN'T WANT TO TAKE THE PLUNGE!
- ☐ THE FISH WHO COULDN'T SWIM!
- ☐ THE HYENA WHO WOULDN'T LAUGH!
- ☐ THE BIRD WHO WAS AFRAID OF HEIGHTS!
- ☐ THE EAGLE WHO DIDN'T WANT TO WEAR HIS GLASSES ANYMORE!
- ☐ AND MORE!